PUPPY LOVE
The Story of Esme and Sam

For my dear New York friends – Simone, Dominic, Max and Jack Ciafardini
GS

For my darling children, Esme and Sam
EH

SIMON AND SCHUSTER

First published in Great Britain in 2008 by Simon & Schuster UK Ltd
Africa House, 64-78 Kingsway, London WC2B 6AH
A CBS COMPANY

Text copyright © 2008 Gillian Shields
Illustrations copyright © 2008 Elizabeth Harbour
The right of Gillian Shields and Elizabeth Harbour to be identified as
the author and illustrator of this work has been asserted by them
in accordance with the Copyright, Designs and Patents Act, 1988

Book designed by Genevieve Webster

A CIP catalogue record for this book is available from
the British Library upon request

ISBN-10: 1 4169 1041 7
ISBN-13: 978 1 4169 1041 1

Printed in China
1 3 5 7 9 10 8 6 4 2

PUPPY LOVE
The Story of Esme and Sam

Gillian Shields & Elizabeth Harbour

SIMON AND SCHUSTER
London New York Sydney

This is the city and this is the park,
Where dogs run and play with a yap and a bark.

Here is the dog called Esme Lamour,
Who lives in a penthouse up on the top floor.

And here is the dog called Samuel Bloom,
Who lives in a crowded tenement room.

Esme has luncheon of chicken and crab,
Samuel eats any scraps he can grab.

Esme reposes on satins and lace,
Samuel sleeps wherever there's space.

Promptly at three Esme walks in the park,
Where Samuel prowls alone when it's dark.
One afternoon, all sunny and bright,
Mrs B Goldstein had such a bad fright:

Esme's pink lead somehow slipped from her collar,
And Mrs B Goldstein started to holler.
But Esme was after some freedom and fun,
So she followed her nose and started to run.

It was all so exciting, so thrilling and new,

Until the day faded and long shadows grew.

Esme barked in a panic and ran all about,

As Mrs B Goldstein continued to shout.

Esme ran to the left, Mrs B to the right!

And quickly, too quickly, the day turned to night.

Mrs B Goldstein went sadly back home,
And called the police on her gold telephone;
"Oh, do find my darling! Send all of your men!
I'll pay a reward – in dollars or yen!"

So poor little Esme was left there to shiver,
Alone in the dark, her heart all a-quiver.
She longed to be back with her mistress so dear –
With kind Mrs B she'd had nothing to fear!

Yet now she was frightened of all she could see,
A horse like a ghost, and a rat, and a tree.
But . . .

. . . Samuel Bloom was coming uptown,

To walk in the park, now the sun had gone down.

Samuel Bloom could put all to right,

Samuel Bloom was the king of the night!

He knew all the paths, he could smell out a rat,

He wasn't afraid of an owl or a bat,

And under a bush, just by the lake,

He found Esme Lamour in a terrible quake.

"Hey kid, what's the problem?" he said. "Don't be down.

You're in the Big Apple – that's my kinda town!"

"But I'm lost," she replied, with a soft, timid smile.

"Follow me," Samuel grinned. "It's less than a mile!"

So he led, and she followed, by lake and by zoo . . .

By grottoes and arbours, where wild roses grew.

They walked and they talked, and a sweet night-bird sang.
They talked and they walked, as the old church bell rang.
He showed her the stars and the great shining moon,
And in Esme's heart, love started to bloom.

She trustingly gazed at Sam's fine hairy muzzle,

As under the stars, they started to nuzzle.

"Oh, darling," she gasped, "can this really be true?"

And that's when he said, "It's true – I love you!"

When dawn came, by Mrs B's splendid front door,
They pledged their true love, for ever, and more.

But old Mrs B didn't see it that way,
She grabbed hold of Esme, and chased Sam away.
"Has that nasty, rough doggy been horrid, my dear?
We'll make sure he doesn't come hanging round here."
And she told Ed, the doorman, in tones firm and strong,
If he ever saw Samuel, "Just move him along!"

So Samuel slipped back to his tenement's gloom,

Unlucky, unhappy, poor Samuel Bloom!

Esme was back with her satins and silk,

Her lobsters and beefsteaks, her eggs and her milk.

But without Samuel Bloom, the world seemed so grey . . .

That Esme Lamour, one day, ran away!
She sped out of the door and into the street,
Before Mrs B Goldstein could utter a bleat.

Downtown she flew, with her heart in her mouth,
It was all strange and new, but she kept heading south.

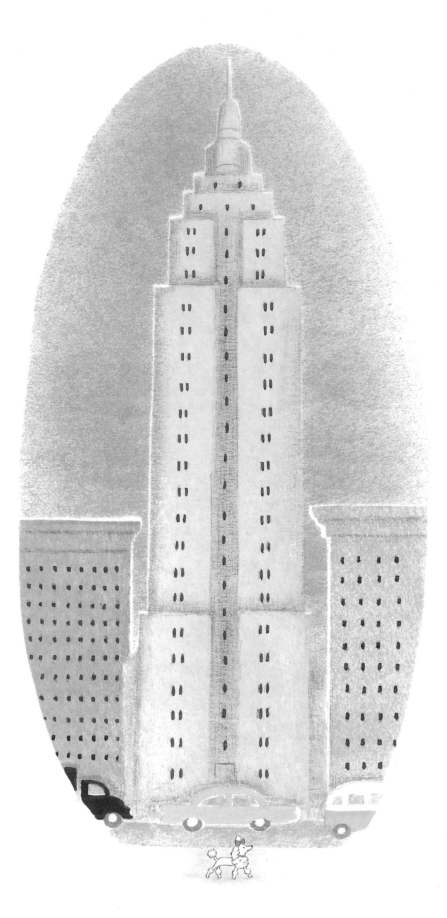

Past buildings so tall, down avenues long,

Her love made her brave, her love made her strong.

Past dark downtown streets, with long traffic jams . . .

Past China, past Italy, past ice-cream and hams . . .

She raced up the steps to that tenement room,
To meet once again with her promised bridegroom.
"Hey, kid!" exclaimed Sam. "Is that you at the door?"
"Yes, darling," she answered, "for ever, and more."

Now this is the city and this is the park,

Where dogs run and play with a yap and a bark.

Promptly at three, rain or shine, every day,

Mrs B Goldstein is walking that way.

And with her walk Esme, and Samuel Bloom,
And five little puppies, as round as the moon.

The End